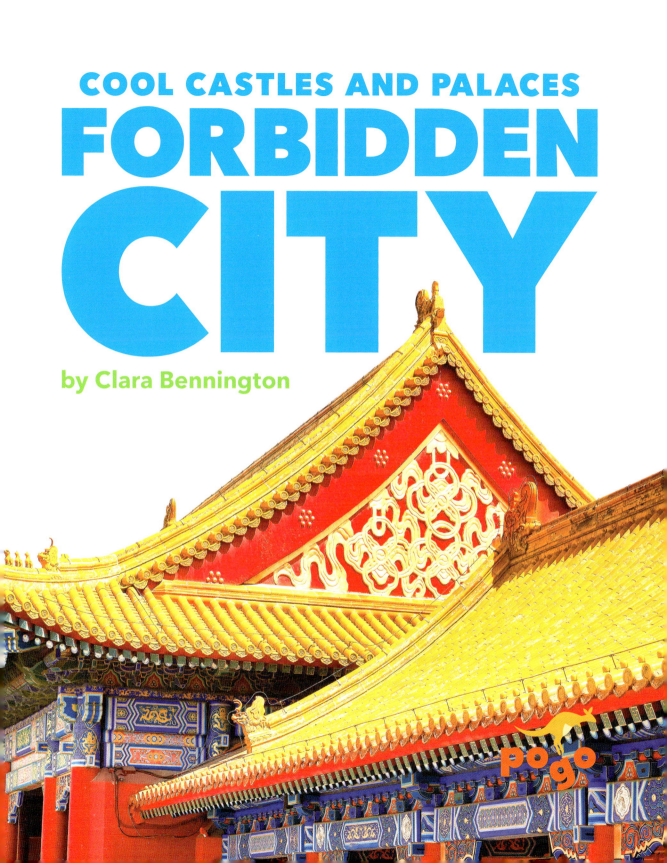

COOL CASTLES AND PALACES
FORBIDDEN CITY

by Clara Bennington

po go

Ideas for Parents and Teachers

Pogo Books let children practice reading informational text while introducing them to nonfiction features such as headings, labels, sidebars, maps, and diagrams, as well as a table of contents, glossary, and index.

Carefully leveled text with a strong photo match offers early fluent readers the support they need to succeed.

Before Reading

• "Walk" through the book and point out the various nonfiction features. Ask the student what purpose each feature serves.

• Look at the glossary together. Read and discuss the words.

Read the Book

• Have the child read the book independently.

• Invite him or her to list questions that arise from reading.

After Reading

• Discuss the child's questions. Talk about how he or she might find answers to those questions.

• Prompt the child to think more. Ask: What did you know about the Forbidden City before you read this book? What more do you want to learn?

Pogo Books are published by Jump!
5357 Penn Avenue South
Minneapolis, MN 55419
www.jumplibrary.com

Library of Congress Cataloging-in-Publication Data

Names: Bennington, Clara, author.
Title: Forbidden City / by Clara Bennington.
Description: Minneapolis, MN: Pogo Books are published by Jump!, 2020.
Series: Cool castles and palaces
Includes index. | Audience: Age 7-10.
Identifiers: LCCN 2018060486 (print)
LCCN 2018061220 (ebook)
ISBN 9781641288668 (ebook)
ISBN 9781641288651 (hardcover : alk. paper)
Subjects: LCSH: Forbidden City (Beijing, China)
Juvenile literature. | China—Kings and rulers
Biography—Juvenile literature.
Classification: LCC DS795.8.F67 (ebook)
LCC DS795.8.F67 B46 2020 (print) | DDC 951/.156—dc23
LC record available at https://lccn.loc.gov/2018060486

Editor: Jenna Trnka
Designer: Molly Ballanger

Photo Credits: gianliguori/iStock, cover; Brian Kinney/Shutterstock, 1; axz700/Shutterstock, 3; Zhao jian kang/Shutterstock, 4; TommL/iStock, 5; Han maomin/Shutterstock, 6-7; superjoseph/Shutterstock, 8-9; Fedor Selivanov/Shutterstock, 10-11; Cassionhabib/Shutterstock, 12; superjoseph/iStock, 13; fuyu liu/Shutterstock, 14-15; Steve Vidler/SuperStock, 16; kudla/Shutterstock, 17; Iconotec/Alamy, 18; RM Asia/Alamy, 18-19; xPACIFICA/Getty, 20-21; Uwe Aranas/Shutterstock, 23.

Printed in the United States of America at Corporate Graphics in North Mankato, Minnesota.

TABLE OF CONTENTS

CHAPTER 1

IMPERIAL PALACE

Welcome to the Forbidden City! It is a palace **complex** in Beijing, China. Great **emperors** once stood on this balcony.

balcony

This palace was home to 24 emperors over 500 years. Yongle was the first to live here in 1420. Puyi was the last in 1912. Why? The Chinese Revolution of 1911 **overthrew** the **imperial** system.

The Forbidden City took 14 years to build. It has 980 buildings! A **moat** and walls protected them. The moat is 170 feet (52 meters) wide. The walls are 32 feet (9.8 m) high. Arrow Towers are at each corner.

Arrow Tower

wall

moat

TAKE A LOOK!

The Forbidden City has a **symmetrical** design. The gates are across from each other. This was for balance. It is known as yin and yang.

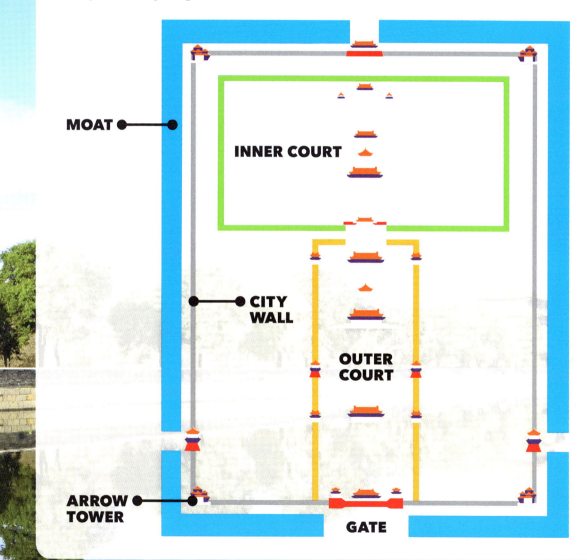

MOAT

INNER COURT

CITY WALL

OUTER COURT

ARROW TOWER

GATE

throne

The Outer Court is where **royal** business took place. Three main halls are here. The Hall of Supreme Harmony is the largest. The **throne** is here. The hall was used for important events. **Coronations** took place here.

DID YOU KNOW?

Why is it called the Forbidden City? Common people were not allowed inside. Even members of the royal family were not free to go inside all of the buildings. Only the ruler could go anywhere he wanted.

The Inner Court was where the royal family lived. Trees and rock gardens fill the Imperial Garden. Two **pavilions** with round roofs are there as well.

pavilion

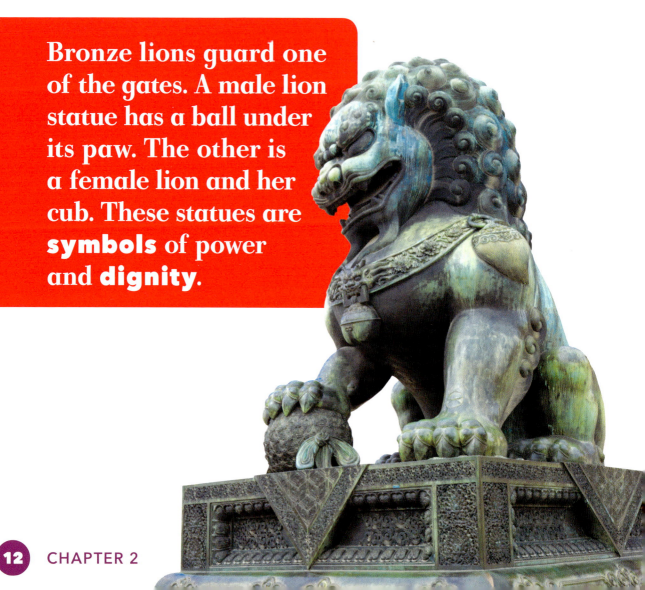

CHAPTER 2

SYMBOLS IN THE CITY

Bronze lions guard one of the gates. A male lion statue has a ball under its paw. The other is a female lion and her cub. These statues are **symbols** of power and **dignity**.

Five marble bridges cross the Golden Water River. They stand for important Chinese **virtues**.

Dragons represent the rulers' power. The throne has a gold dragon on it. Dragons are found on many buildings here, too.

WHAT DO YOU THINK?

The number nine is believed to be very lucky in China. Nine times nine was especially lucky. Do you think numbers can be lucky? Do you have a lucky number?

9

CHAPTER 3

PALACE MUSEUM

China's rulers surrounded themselves with beautiful objects. Almost two million items that belonged to them are still here!

The palace opened as a museum in 1925. Why? People could learn more about life here.

Visitors can see a marble ramp carved with dragons. It weighs more than 550,000 pounds (250 metric tons)! How did such a heavy item get here? Roads were flooded in the winter to form ice. It was moved along the ice!
You can see paintings and **artifacts**, too.

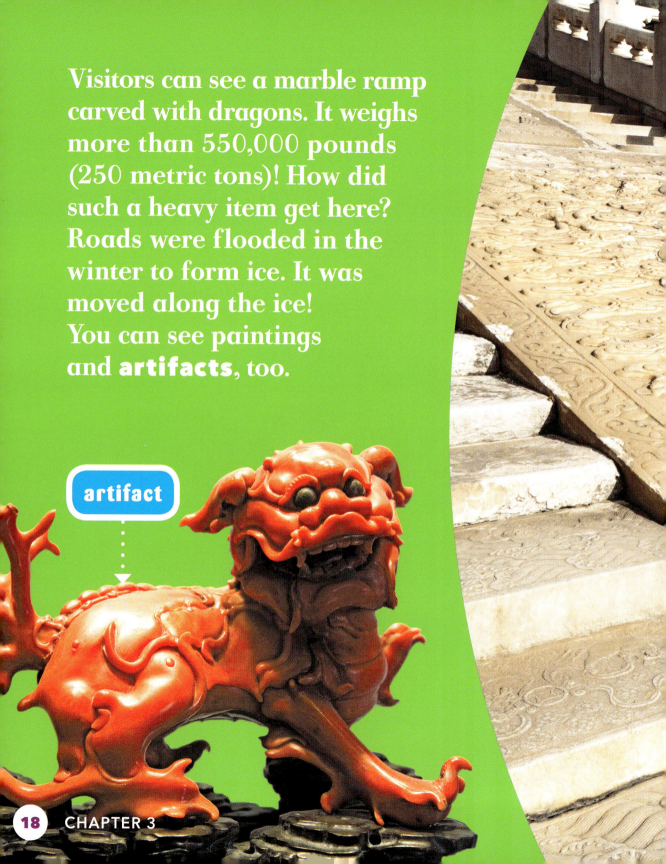

artifact

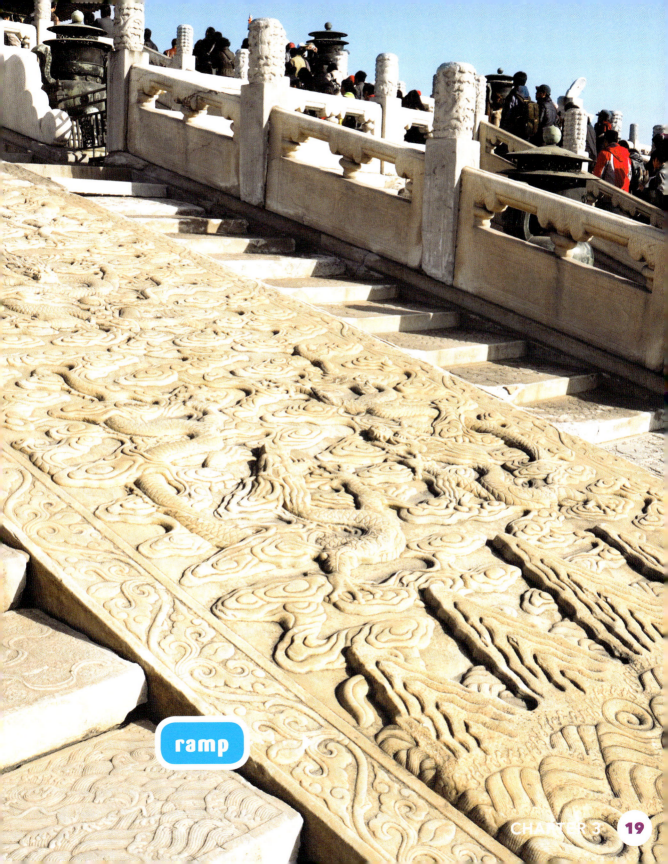

ramp

The palace used to be forbidden. But now all are welcome here. You can learn more about how China's great rulers once lived. Would you like to visit?

WHAT DO YOU THINK?

Many valuable objects were given away by the last ruler. Some were lost. Do you think people who have them should return them to the museum?

QUICK FACTS & TOOLS

FORBIDDEN CITY

Location: Beijing, China

Years Built: 1406–1420

Size: 178 acres (72 hectares)

Number of Buildings: 980

Number of Rooms: 9,999

Current Use: Palace Museum

Average Number of Visitors Each Day: 80,000

GLOSSARY

artifacts: Objects made or changed by human beings and used in the past.

complex: A group of buildings that are near each other and are used for similar purposes.

coronations: Ceremonies in which kings, queens, or other rulers are crowned.

dignity: A quality that makes a person worthy of honor or respect.

emperors: Male rulers of an empire. An empire is a group of countries or states that has the same ruler.

imperial: Of or having to do with an empire.

moat: A deep, wide ditch dug around a castle and filled with water to prevent enemy attacks.

overthrew: To have put an end to something or to have forced someone from power.

pavilions: Open buildings that are used for shelter or recreation.

royal: Related to a king or queen or a member of his or her family.

symbols: Objects or designs that stand for, suggest, or represent something else.

symmetrical: Having matching points, parts, or shapes on both sides of a dividing line.

throne: A special chair for a ruler to sit on during a ceremony.

virtues: Good qualities. The five virtues the marble bridges stand for are charity, honesty, knowledge, integrity, and politeness.

INDEX

TO LEARN MORE

Finding more information is as easy as 1, 2, 3.

1. Go to www.factsurfer.com
2. Enter "ForbiddenCity" into the search box.
3. Choose your book to see a list of websites.

FACT SURFER